P9-DMA-288

Sisters of Glass

Also by Stephanie Hemphill

Your Own, Sylvia

Sisters
of
Glass

STEPHANIE HEMPHILL

EMBER

For my little sister, Kate

This is a work of fiction. Names, characters, places, and incidents either are the product of the author's imagination or are used fictitiously. Any resemblance to actual persons, living or dead, events, or locales is entirely coincidental.

Text copyright © 2012 by Stephanie Hemphill
Cover art copyright © 2012 by Anna and Elena Balbusso

All rights reserved. Published in the United States by Ember, an imprint of Random House Children's Books, a division of Random House, Inc., New York. Originally published in hardcover in the United States by Alfred A. Knopf, an imprint of Random House Children's Books, New York, in 2012.

Ember and the E colophon are registered trademarks of Random House, Inc.

Visit us on the Web! randomhouse.com/teens

Educators and librarians, for a variety of teaching tools, visit us at RHTeachersLibrarians.com

Library of Congress Cataloging-in-Publication Data is available upon request.

ISBN 978-0-307-98141-7 (pbk.)

RL: 6.0

Printed in the United States of America

10 9 8 7 6 5 4 3 2 1

First Ember Edition 2013

Random House Children's Books supports the First Amendment and celebrates the right to read.

AUTHOR'S NOTE

In 1487, the real Maria Barovier, daughter of Angelo Barovier, received permission from the Doge to build a little furnace on Murano for the firing of enamels. She was one of the few women glassmakers of the time and the first known to be granted permission to build her own furnace. This small historical detail inspired me to write this book.

SECOND DAUGHTER

I feel Giovanna's fire
as Mother prepares me for suitors,
polishes me
while Giovanna polishes glass.

Though I am the younger daughter
and rightfully should *not* marry
into Venetian nobility,
my father declared
the day I was born,
the week he invented cristallo,
that I was his
baby of good fortune,
and good fortune would be mine.
I would marry a senator.

Yet like tides washed into shore
by winds one never sees,
we all prayed
he would change his mind.
We were thus raised
to follow tradition.

Giovanna shoots me
only a sideways glance
as I lace into my new green dress.

I want to scream,
"I will trade positions,"
that I desire to polish glass
and stoke the fires
and see the creation of crystal,
like I was permitted to do
when I was a little girl.

But I promised Father
on his deathbed that I would
honor his first and greatest wish for me.
I just did not know I would
lose my sister even before
I lose my Murano.

MY FATHER, ANGELO BAROVIER

The Barovier family furnace
has molded glass on Murano
for nearly two hundred years, since 1291,
when the Venetian government
required that all furnaces move
to my island home.
The Council of Ten claimed
that it was to prevent fires.
But containing all glassmakers
on Murano also allowed Venice to regulate
her most profitable industry
and to prevent leakage of trade secrets
beyond Venetian shores.

My father spent his entire life
on Murano, never once sailing
into the ocean, not even to Venice.
Father said, "Ships are for cargo,
what need have I of them?"
Besides, he sailed
the vast ocean of his mind,
so indeed, he traveled everywhere.

Father studied to be the scholar
of his family and was to attend
the University of Padua.
My uncle Giova says
he never saw one so eager
to see the world, that my father
packed his bags for university
two weeks in advance.

But fire overtook
one of the two Barovier fornicas
like a thunderstorm.

My father lost his father,
his mother, three of his brothers,
and his only sister
to the torrent of flames.

Father unfolded his clothes.
He and his one remaining brother, Giova,
found work at neighboring furnaces
until they saved enough ducats
to purchase materials for their own.

I always wondered why
my father did not fear
the furnace and the flame,
the hot molten cullet.
He said, "Dearest Maria,
does a general fear a battle
after he loses men on the field?
No. He studies what went wrong,
resolves it, and fights better the next time.
Otherwise, the loss of his soldiers was in vain."

Not one day
did my father miss work,
even holy days
he created his batches
sundown to dawn.
Angelo Barovier carried
the deaths in his family
on his shoulders
like a mule never relieved
of his load.

I am named Maria
after his sister, who died.

My father died
when I was ten.
Mother wore clothes of mourning
for five years,
until she determined
it was time
to begin grooming me
to be bartered away
from my home.

THE GLASS VESSEL

In some prominent glassmakers' homes
girls do not work with glass at all,
but my father raised us
to be a family of industry,
all of his children schooled
to understand the art
and business of the Baroviers.

Like first mates to the captain,
we all learned
to prepare ingredients,
to stoke the thousand-degree furnace
with beech and alder wood,
to make his frit,
to polish glass,
and even to blow it.
Giovanna and I
have never been permitted
to blow a punty,
but we understand
how it works.

A well-run vessel,
we naturally settled
into our rightful crew positions.
Father steered and guided the ship.
He remained inventor.
I became his assistant,
lagged after him like a dog,
bobbled carefully
the ingredients for his batch.

My brother Paolo
has blown glass for the Doge,
a master gaffer
my father never saw rivaled.

My eldest brother, Marino,
like my uncle Giova,
dove into business affairs
as though he had been handling
the wicked waves of supply and demand
for a thousand years.

Giovanna and Mother,
both experts at beautification,
polish glass so that our wares
sparkle finer than crown jewels,
so we deliver the premier glass on Murano.

Always servants, hired hands,
workers from other guilds
swabbed decks of the Barovier ship,
for the workload was too great
to bear just us six.

For seven years our two furnaces
alone produced cristallo,
the secret recipe for colorless glass
hidden in the bow of our ship.

But Paolo and Marino
believe that because
Father was stubborn
as a wheel stuck in mud,
our secret escaped.

Father refused to outsource work,
he rather brought laborers into
the Barovier fornicas,
and one must have spied
when Father and I prepared a batch.

Within two weeks
all the major furnaces on Murano
produced cristallo.

We no longer
sat first in church.

Paolo unsheathed his sword
to slay everyone
who worked in our kiln.

Father disarmed him.
"You cannot kill
all the innocent
to avenge the guilty *one*."

But after his recipe dispersed,
my father lost
the jaunt to his step
and seemed always
to press a hand over his heart.

A year later
we buried my father at sea.
Clutching a clear cristallo cross,
he departed Murano
for the first time,
never to return.

TALENT

A graceless gosling,
I stumble through most things.
Like a baby just learning to walk,
I try to step forward
on my own but usually
fall down bottom-heavy.

Giovanna excels without even trying,
as though she emerged
from the womb a golden child—
fair, gentle, kindhearted, feminine,
and she sings sweeter, and with better tone,
than the finest instrument.
Her voice could praise the Doge,
her singing make God weep.

As she polishes glass
or if gloom fogs the day,
Vanna will step to the window
and sing to lift those who labor
with melody and cheer.
People cease working
and listen. Some deliberately
route past our palazzo
to hear her music.

My voice sounds old
and witchy as crackling flames.

One day Vanna sang
little rippling scales
out the window, and the light
on her hair and cheeks
made her look like a saint.
I grabbed paper and quill

from my father's old work desk
and drew Giovanna in her radiance,
sketched how she made us all feel
when we heard her voice.

She cried when I showed her the drawing.
I started to tear apart the page.
"I'm sorry, Vanna.
I didn't mean to hurt your feelings."

"Stop! Give me that."
She ran downstairs to find
Marino and Paolo and Mother.

I ran after her, but of course she
could surpass me
without losing a breath.
I tumbled down the stairs
as the tears slipped down my cheeks.

Everyone walled around me.
"I am sorry. I meant it to be nice."
My tears turned to sobs.

Mother stroked my head.
"Look at me, Maria. I wish
your father could have seen this."
She hugged me closer
than she had in a year.
"But then, he always said
you were more of an artist
than a cristallo chef."

The next day Marino
presented me
my first sketchbook.

HOW TO BEGIN?

A large sheet of white,
pen and brown ink in hand—
my mind deserted me.
I shivered in summer sunlight.
Mother relieved me
of my morning chores
so that I could practice sketching,
and my hand cramped up.

Giovanna skipped back
into our room to grab
her second pair of work gloves.
I stared at her, hoping
she would sense my distress
and offer a light amidst my fog,
a beacon to save my ship
the rocky shore.

She scurried to leave
without an eye in my direction.
I squawked, "Giovanna, come here."

"What, Maria? Mother expects me,"
she said as she swirled swanlike
over to where I perched on my bed.
"You have not drawn anything
this whole morning?"

"It is not for lack of will.
I can't think what to draw.
I am a failure.
I must not be an artist after all."
A few tears splattered my paper.

"No, no." Vanna squeezed my hand.
"You are thinking too much.
Just draw what you see,
what is around you,
and how it makes you feel,
just like you drew me."

She brushed her finger
over my lips and cheeks
in the shape of a smile.
"And be joyful as you do it.
Father always said,
'A sad gaffer produces gloomy glass,
whereas a happy one creates crystal.' "

"I think you are the artist, Vanna."

"No, I am many things, but not that."
And my sister streamed off,
a wake of notes in her trail.

I shut my eyes.
When I opened them
the room tripled in size.
I drew my sister's bed, her vanity.
I inked her painting a smile across my face.
Before the afternoon I completed
eight sketches, each one more improved
than the last. I showed Vanna my work.
"Bella," she said.

I crammed my first sketchbook with joy.
Not all drawings of happy subjects,
but all penned in gratitude
and excitement—
my brothers at work,
the cathedral, a fisherman

I gleaned through the window,
our maid Carlotta rolling out dough,
the *conciatore* preparing our frit,
Mother at her dressing table,
Giovanna's brush and comb
from her perspective,
Paolo blowing his glass art;
I recorded it all.

WHY I LOVE GLASS

Giovanna loves glass
like she loves singing,
because like a melody
she enhances its beauty
with her touch.

Marino loves glass
because his investment
brings prosperity and growth.
As with a gardener,
his well-managed, well-tended furnace
produces great fruit.

Paolo creates himself
in each goblet, beaker, bowl
he blows. He cannot really see
himself without his reflection
in the glass's eye.

Uncle Giova knows nothing
but glass; it is his past, present,
and future—the fornica
is his home.

I love glass
because I love my father.
After Father died
I worked like a nun
to prepare his sacred batches.
My father stood beside me;
his specter guided my hand.
"Maria, not too much manganese."

After we lost him,
I turned to glass.

Mother turned away from it.
She shrouded goblets and mirrors;
we drank from clay.

At first I did not understand.
But one day, thinking about my father,
I held up a mirror
and saw my mother's eyes.

RESTRICTED

At fifteen all doors
began to lock around me.
I could hear the turning keys.
I pounded on the walls.
No one told me why
I had to stay inside my room.
Had I mistreated the glass
I so loved? No.
What had I done?

Giovanna finally explained,
"You must be a lady
if you hope to marry a senator."

She eyed me then as never before,
like men I witnessed about to duel.
"If it is *possible* for you to be a lady.
And if not, well then perhaps . . ."

Vanna's eyes shifted back
to the sister I knew.
"Maria, is it not enough
that Father loved you best?"
But before her tears
she turned away.

For the past several months
I have been treated
more delicately
than the Doge's chandelier.
My complexion
to remain powder white, hands smooth
and clean, no ink tainting my nails.

My virtue must be as the purest cristallo;
I can go nowhere unchaperoned.
All the while my sister's silent sorrow
thrusts glass shards into my heart.

GIOVANNA

My sister's long golden locks
glimmer in sunlight;
how her crown of hair
would jewel in Venice
away from Murano's fire and ash.
She labors morning and night
to brush away this island's soot.

When I was fourteen and Vanna
was fifteen, we decided to play
a trick on our older brothers,
Marino and Paolo.
We bound each other's hands,
moaned as though we had burned
ourselves stoking the furnace.

Marino's tan turned to salt.
He said, "You must stay inside
and apply the treatment."
Paolo plugged his nose.
The treatment, a muddy goop
our maid Carlotta prepares,
consists primarily of dung.
But it salves wounds.

As soon as the boys set to their tasks,
Giovanna declared,
"The day is too beautiful to stay inside,"
and whisked me away faster than a fierce gale
fuels clouds through the sky.

Murano's streets curve and twist
like eels. We might have been
lost in the smoke of all the fornicas.
But the sun owned Murano

that day, the sky colored like the sea,
no rain in view. And Vanna
seemed to know where she was going.

I might have been afraid we would
get in trouble for being out,
two girls alone, but none seemed to notice.
Merchants bartered glass to boatmen.
Citizens swam through the streets
with great haste, as though they fled from fire.

Vanna serpentined me
down an alley past the cathedral
to a small shop. Inside, a painting
of Venice's Grand Canal
hung quietly on the wall.
Meticulous in its detail,
but it somehow felt dead.
The painting celebrated the holy day
Corpus Christi and the procession
through the Piazza San Marco,
but it was as though the painter
felt not the joy of his subject
nor the joy of his creation.

Giovanna tugged my arm.
"They have charcoal and red chalk,
pink paper, just like the painters use.
I thought you might like—"

I cut her off. "I have heard of these,
but I have no coin."

She pulled a bolognini from her sleeve.

I whispered, "Where did you get that?
We will be robbed."

Vanna shook her head.
"You worry too much, Maria.
Select what you like.
I will manage the rest."

I hugged her tight enough to crack
her bones. "I'll pay you back."

She smiled. "Yes, you will."

NOT MY MOTHER'S DAUGHTER

I spend my days now
with a woman I do not understand.
It is as though Mother speaks French.

She presents to me a carved wooden box
painted with fine water lilies.
I turn it around in the light.
"This is exquisite," I say.
"Thank you, Mother.
I will store my inks and quills
in here!" I move to kiss her cheek.

Mother waves me away.
She says, "No, open it up.
The gift is inside."

A silver brush and comb,
far more expensive than any
Giovanna has owned,
lie like weapons
in the velvet-lined box.

"Vanna will love these."
I say aloud what I meant
to keep in my head.

Mother squawks at me
like an angry goose.
"No. They are for you.
They were my grandmother's.
You alone will use them
to brush your hair
one hundred times each day."

Oh, Vanna will hate me if she sees these.
This brush and comb belong to her
like limbs extending from her wrist.
Her name should be engraved
on the handles.
The box alone feels like mine.

Dear Lord, why did Father
disturb tradition?

"Mother, this is better suited
for Vanna," I begin,
but like my sister
Mother's ears sew closed to my voice.
She directs me from her room.

If Father were here,
at least I could speak to him
about all of this.
Mother is like Murano's stone wall,
impenetrable.
I know not
how to reason with stone,
only to crush it,
and I cannot do that.

THE BRUSH-OFF

I sneak the box into our room
and nestle it behind my dresses.
How I will stroke my hair
one hundred times
without Giovanna noticing,
I cannot fathom!

Giovanna wakes me
just as the sun eases
above the sea.
She holds the painted box.
"Where did you get this?"

"It is a gift for you from Mother.
I was supposed to hide it from you."

Giovanna looks as though
she might sing.
"I must thank her right away.
The brush and comb set
is so beautiful, exquisitely
beautiful!"

"No." I grab her arm.

"I don't understand."
She shakes her head.

"Well, you see—" I begin.

"No, I don't. Tell the truth.
On the Virgin Mary's soul,
is the brush set yours or mine?"
Giovanna's eyes slay me.

I look down. "They are mine."
But then quickly add,
"But they should be yours.
I give them to you."

"No." Giovanna sinks.
"You cannot do that."

She squares herself away from me,
sets the box on my dresser,
and her voice falls dumb.

SECRET SKETCHINGS

Drawing emotional pictures
is whimsical child's play;
I am to pack my pencils, inks,
and tablets away.
All the scenes of craftsmen
in the rain, furnace flames,
the canal, cathedral, glass boats,
and portraits of my family
that Mother so adored
she tucks under her bed
as though she buries me
beneath her mattress.

"I thought it was customary
for a girl to have talent?"
I ask Mother as she peels
the last sketchbook she can find
from my arms.

"No, Maria," Mother corrects.
"You should have an amusement.
So, yes, you shall say that you draw,
and draw the nobleman in his glory
or other lovely things like flowers,
but none of this art
that looks like a man might have drawn it."

PAOLO AND THE COURTESAN

Across the Grand Canal
on the weedy side of Murano,
Father said the mermaidens
reign. Beautiful temptresses
who cast out golden nets
and snare many fish.
Father never swam there,
but Uncle Giova
still fills his pockets
with glass bracelets
and comes home after moonrise
more than once a week.
Once my uncle left
a set of jade combs
on Giovanna's dresser.
Another morning
I found a sketchbook
filled with drawings
of ladies in fine attire
looking into mirrors.
Masterful drawings
in terms of light
and perspective.
I learned to draw
in spatial dimensions
studying this book.
"Who drew these?"
I asked Uncle.
He whispered in my ear,
"A beautiful woman."
I nodded.
"A siren of the sea."

My ears identify the click
of Paolo's boots as dawn blinks
through the window.
He wears last night's cloak.
Sea perfume wafts up the stairs
like the scent of baking bread,
the same aroma flavoring
the sketchbook
Uncle bestowed upon me.

Paolo arrives late to the furnace,
and when he sets to leave before
dusk, Marino stomps after him.
"Your goblets today are shoddy."

They bicker like boatmen
about to draw swords,
loud voices in the street
for all the neighborhood ears.

Paolo shoves his pontil
into Marino's hands.
"Do it yourself, then."

Paolo steers our gondola
quickly toward the weeds,
vanishes into the smoke
and fog for three days.

Our furnace produces
no glass in Paolo's absence;
the orders for English betrothal goblets
pile up like debtor's notes.

Paolo returns, biretta in hand,
and kneels before Mother's tears.
He kisses her glove.
"I am sorry, Mother, forgive me,
but this is too much alone.
Gaffing cannot be all that I do."

"I know, my son."
She pats his head.
"I will speak with Marino."

LEARNING TO BE A LADY

is like learning
to live within a shell,
to be a crustacean encased
in a small white
uncomfortable world.
You hear the ocean
whirl about you
but feel not the wet
nor ride the wave
nor see the sun.

Bedded on the sand,
protected from harm
with the other fair dainty shells,
all safely collected
so no damage be done
to precious contents.
I cannot venture outside my cage,
cannot dirty my gloves.

This was not how Father
raised me, some fragile figurine
teetering on the ledge—
how can this be his greatest
wish for me?
Did he not think me capable of more?

My cheeks red as a fornica,
I fall to my knees.
"Hail Mary, full of grace,
forgive me my insolence and disrespect.
I do not mean to be so ungrateful.
Giovanna would shear her head
to be in my position. I am blessed
to be of such good fortune."

MY INSOLENCE STARVES MY FAMILY

Marino's hands wring tightly
at the supper table;
he never says it,
but I know an influx of ducats
would fuel the second furnace
and hire additional hands.

If I marry well, then Marino
may take a wife
and acquire a large dowry
for our family.

I will suck in my ribs
while Mother bodices me
into my corset.
I will see my pinching shoes as fins.

I announce at the table,
"We shall settle on my proper
suitor, all of us, before
I turn sixteen."

Mother pushes back her
plate and beaker.
"We have much work ahead."

TRIAL BY FIRE: FIRST SUITOR

"You shall learn by doing,"
Mother determines, "for we have
precious little time.
The Barovier name was worth
a lot more a few years ago."

Traditionally girls do not meet
with men. Fathers arrange
marriages, or heads of families do,
but Marino and Uncle
are more frenzied than netted sharks,
and Mother and I cannot leave Murano
to attend parties and meet noble ladies
with eligible sons, so we break
tradition and invite bachelors
approved by my brothers
into our home to visit Mother and me.

Fastened into a puffy-sleeved
blue velvet gown,
a tiara smashed into my skull,
I feel costumed into noble
clothes like I should sport
a carnival mask.

I peer out the window;
the gondola he arrives in
nearly capsizes
when the rotund man exits it.

"Giovanna, come see," I say,
and then remember
she refuses to talk to me.

I clutch the wall as I descend
the stairs so I do not topple
in these tall shoes.

I feel like I ate old fish,
know immediately
from his foul breath
that I cannot marry this man.

He coughs and squints
with an upturned nose.
"How old is she?"

Mother offers,
"Would you like to come in
and rest your feet, Signore Debratto?"

He stomps his cane.
"Her! How old is she?"
His face reddens from the exertion.

"I am fifteen, sir," I say.

Mother bites her lip; apparently
I was not to speak.

But since I already spilled the tea,
I ask him, "How old are you?"

Signore Debratto huffs and grumbles.
"Well, I told your son I needed
a *young* wife," he says to Mother.

He lifts his cane and raises my hair
to inspect behind my ears.
I hide behind my mother.
"Well, since she is so old,

I'll expect a larger dowry."
Signore Debratto wobbles in our doorway.

"I believe you may be right, sir.
Maria may be too mature for your tastes."
Mother clasps my hand
and directs me upstairs
as our maid Carlotta
swiftly locks the door
behind my first suitor.

"Did he have a stench
about him?" Mother asks.

"Indeed," I say, and
we collapse in laughter,
and Mother feels
like a friend
for the first time.

GIOVANNA'S SONGS

disappear like raindrops
into the sea. Only sad notes
sob against her pillow at night.

This morning I want to say,
"Isn't it a beautiful day?"
or "Can I help you shine
that bowl?" I clear my throat
of its toads and attempt to hum,
but my melody is a boorish grunt.
I ask Vanna, "Can you sing
that hymn from Mass?"

Giovanna spears me
with one sharp "No."
A fish so dead I cannot flail
but slump to my bed,
my eyes spin blank and glassy.
Who stole my sister, and why?

I tiptoe to the window
in my large straw hat.
People gather below
and point up at me.
A woman shakes
her head. "No, it's not her."
And they all stride on.

"What's wrong with you?"
I raise my voice like
a high fierce wind.
"I will go away,
but must you punish them?"
I gesture to the street below.

Vanna widens her lips;
a scratchy sound
like a poorly bowed violin
escapes her throat.
"I cannot sing."
She turns from me,
weeping into her hands.
"There's something from hell about me."

I shake my head. "No."
I try to garland my arms
around her neck.

"Do not touch me."
Giovanna brandishes
her brush as a club.
"You have cursed me already.
Just leave me alone."

I wanted to share
my story of the awful Debratto
with her, but I guess I will be solo
on this, only Mother to guide me.

OUR FAMILY NEEDS HELP

Marino clasps Mother's hands.
I know I should return
to my bedchamber,
that the scene in the parlor
is private, but my feet
smolder into the floor.

"Paolo cannot handle
all of our orders.
He spends hours a day
with that courtesan Beatrice,
bewitched by her swooshing skirts.
He has lost focus."
Marino inhales, then blows
out his breath
like he was working a punty.
"There is a gaffer all the families
bid to attain right now named Luca.
Giova believes if we sell off
our second fornica we might secure him."
Marino looks at Mother
as if he were a child of five.
He kneels and kisses her hands.

Mother shakes her head.
"Your father asked me never to sell
the second furnace."

"But we cannot afford materials,
cannot staff it; the kilns
are in disrepair." Marino sighs.
"I do not want to sell it either,
but what else can we do?"

Mother rises and purses her lips.
"What if we give this Luca
a piece of the business,
make him half owner
of the second furnace
instead of selling it?"

"Make him, who comes
from the lower labor class,
like one of our family?"
Marino shakes his head.
"That could be dangerous.
Luca may not hold the same
respect for our family name
and business."

I inch down the stairs.
Uncle Giova, silent as a chalice,
eyes the action from a corner chair.

Uncle finally speaks.
"On the other hand,
giving Luca a sizable stake
in our fornica
could build loyalty.
I am not sure he will receive
such offers from other families,
seeing as he has no known background.
Your mother's plan has merit.
I will propose this to Luca."

Marino pounds the table,
but then like the sky
after thunder and illumination,
he stills and quiets.

"Let it stand that I was against
this plan, but I will do my all
to make it work."

Mother hugs her son.
"Let me speak to Paolo.
I will present this as a gift
not a dagger."

All heads nod.

I turn and scamper up the stairs.
Giovanna glares down at me
with a wicked toothy grin.
"Maria, why are you standing
there on the stairs?" she says
so it echoes.

TROUBLE

My sister's spite
poisons my veins.

Mother banishes me
to the tower of my room.
I must pray my prayer beads
all day because my ears
burned to hear
what they should not.

But worse,
Mother speaks to me
like a child not her own,
no camaraderie in her tone.

Giovanna never tattled on me,
rattled her tail,
spit venom in my face, before.
But because I must marry?

I grab her favorite brush,
dangle it out the window.
It would fragment
should I release it.

Vanna would do this to me.

But I cannot let it go.
I lay the brush on her vanity
and open my armoire.
What I want to do
is melt these dresses
in the fornica!
I want my sister back.
I long to tell her about Luca,

not have her delight
because I am a caged bird—
with nothing to see but old men,
with nothing to do, nothing I can draw,
and no one to talk to.

I yank my hair
and soak my pillow
in a storm of tears.

Mother's scalding eyes,
so disappointed.
Will she trust me again?

And really,
what is wrong with *me*?
Why can't I just do
what my father wanted?

SECOND SUITOR

A tall man with a speckled beard
and a senator's crimson cloak
gaits up our walk
as though he were heralded
into our home like a duke.
He sniffs the air,
brushes off his coat,
and his manservant
hands my mother
a box of oranges and pears
from the Far East.
I peer into the box;
the oranges are the size
of a baby's hand.

"My family, as you may know,
trades silks," Signore Langestora explains.
"I am in charge of the shades
of blue we purchase. I will send
you over a bolt of our latest azure
so that Maria may have a dress made
for the next time we meet."

Mother smiles at each word
that spits forth from this man's mouth.
She did not heed my father as attentively.

Never once does Signore Langestora
glance in my direction;
it is as though he courts Mother.
I suppose this is customary.
I seal my mouth,
do not want to disgrace my family.

A sand martin flutters outside,
beating her wings against the pane glass

as though she wishes to be let in.
At first I want to signal her away,
far away from our house,
let her know that in this place
she will feel trapped
by the ceilings and closed doors.

But the bird flits foolishly at the window,
tired of the wind and waves,
looking for a cage inside
our warm safe home.
She wishes to land, not
hop from one branch to the next,
endlessly hungry.

"Maria would see the world,"
Signore Langestora says,
"as we would spend half the year at sea.
I assume she is accustomed to travel?"

"Well, actually"—Mother hesitates—
"she has never left Murano."

"Fifteen and never off this little island?"
He slaps his thigh with a laugh.
"Well, we will test her sea legs, then.
I will be back in three days
to discuss the arrangements
with Marino and Giova."
He kisses Mother's hands,
nods to me,
readjusts his cloak and hat,
and exits.

I understand most business transactions,
but what just transpired
I cannot quite comprehend.

THE ARRIVAL OF LUCA

No procession with banners
or festival of boats,
but Carlotta prepares a feast
worthy of the Podesta,
the political leader of Murano—
appetizers of grapes, figs, and
Berlingozzo, followed by courses
of pigeon with trout, veal with sausage,
and my favorite, capon.
My stomach squeals
for the dishes to be served,
though this new-fashioned corset
with its tightly laced strings
will scarcely allow me
to *sample* each one.

I peek out my window
like a curious bird
twisting her head halfway round
until my neck strains.
Giovanna just brushes her hair.

I expect trumpets to sound,
doors to unhinge,
but we are simply called to meal,
as our guest has arrived.

Luca's back reveals
a craftsman's brown cloak,
nothing to note;
still, the twenty-two-year-old
ruffles his shoulders and awaits
Uncle's servile assistance
with his drapings
as though Uncle were his manservant,

when properly it is Luca
who should kneel
to my uncle.

My uncle handles Luca's cape
as Marino presents Giovanna and me,
but Luca pays kinder eyes
to the canal rats.

So as Luca and all swivel round,
I thrust my tongue at Luca's better side.

Preparations for this meal
three days in the making,
and our guest offers no comment
on the food or glassware we serve.
We ought to pour him dog urine.

"Did you not like your capon, Luca?"

"I found it salty."
He snubs his piggish nose
and searches the table
for the source of the question.

"What you taste is thyme,"
I say, before I can consider
practicing decorum.

And after consideration
I determine God
will forgive me.

"And rosemary,"
he says, and stands.
"Who is speaking?"

I rise and curtsy.

Luca's gray eyes whirl.

Mother's voice lashes.
"Maria, apologize now!
Then take your leave."

I pick up my skirts
with verve and clamor,
but I hold quiet my tongue.

Whether or not
Mother forgives me.

TIDES OF IMPORT

Mother forgets to be angry
with me,
because like an ocean claiming the beach
at high tide,
Luca moves into and then overtakes
the second fornica
as though it belongs only to him.
Marino wears
a mask of I-told-you-so,
until he realizes
Mother's nerves leave her faint.

Uncle Giova
tells Mother not to worry so much,
that tides shift back.

I overhear her frantic
"But at the speed he is producing glass,
Luca will raise money
to open the second fornica within months.
I am beginning to regret
that I did not heed Marino and keep the business
within our family alone.
Perhaps I disrespect Angelo's wishes in this way."
Mother bites her lower lip.

"Even so." Uncle hushes her. "Please,
do not
let your children catch wind of your fears."

So instead
Mother obsesses over
"Where is the bolt of azure silk
Signore Langestora promised?"
Did the boat capsize?

Did Carlotta's ears miss
the knock of delivery?
Mother paces the front hall
like a hungry seabird
combing the shore for scraps,
back and forth,
    back and forth.

I inch down the stairs.
Mother's head hangs limp
as wet clothes on a line.
"Where is he?"
Mother asks my brothers.

Paolo snaps,
"I would have taken up
swords with him,
but Signore Langestora
is missing as frost in heat."

Marino adds,
"He has likely sailed
to the East. Wherever he is,
he does not intend
to honor his word."

"I had hoped this was settled,"
Mother says to Marino.
"But we shall have to start all over."

"Do not fret," Marino says.
"It will be an easier task
now that Luca is here.
His work is as fine as they say,
and he produces pieces
as fast as lightning
branches the sky.

A true genius, I tell you.
Paolo and I can interview
noblemen for Maria tomorrow
and with more care."

Marino offers Mother his kerchief.
"Oh no, I shed no tears over
that Signore Langestora
and his false promises.
He shall regret not marrying my daughter."

I'd sooner swallow glass
than marry that thin-nosed fish-eye
or any man who insults my family.

MY ESCAPE

So I am not wanted
by a man of crimson cloak
or my sister;
why should I care?

I am hard as glass,
and any dare break me
or cross me
shall be cut.

I sneak past my mother
and my brothers,
refuse the prison of my room.

I trail the servants who stoke
the furnace fires,
their arms choked with wood.
They hasten me away.

None permit me near the flames,
but I wait, patient as a monk.
And when the servants saunter away
I unlatch the furnace door.
Luca alone stands within,
and he waves me inside.

A BRIEF RESPITE

"You are quite dressed
for the furnace this morning,"
Luca says without lifting his eyes.
Why does he not address me
like the lady I am, as he should?

I feel my cheeks begin to ire pink
but will not be flustered.
I brush my hands
on my new velvet petticoat.
"Yes, well, Mother and I were to—
oh, never you mind.
Where is Paolo?"
I ask the question
though I know well
my brother is at the palazzo.

Luca shrugs and beckons me forth.
I might turn and run
or disobey him out of spite,
but the furnace fire
warms me,
and in his work clothes
Luca loses a hint of his bitter smell.

"Maria, bring me the pincers."
Luca stretches out his hand.
"Unless you are too fair
for such work."

Why I fasten on an apron
I can't exactly say.
Perhaps it is because Luca
has remembered my name,

but more likely it is lack
of anything better to do.

I smack the tool into his palm.
"What are you making?"

Luca spins toward me
with his half-finished work.
"A betrothal glass.
It will be sent to the enameler
after this for decoration."

Even though the stem
is yet to be completed,
the goblet Luca molds
is the flawless blue of deep ocean.
I step away from the fires
but cannot peel my eyes
from his work.

"What do you think they will mark
upon the glass?" Luca asks.

"How should I know?" I say.
I feel steamy and wipe my brow
with my apron.

"I thought you were the one
preparing to be married, Maria?"
he says with a smile that feels as
though he has knifed me to the wall.

This causes me to redden.
I begin to say, "How dare you presume
to know everything about—"

A shock of thunder cracks above us,
followed by heavy pounding on the roof.

I can waste not another word,
for the rain falls in waves.
And if my petticoat is soaked and stained of soot,
Mother will surely hail down upon me.

CAUGHT IN THE RAIN

The rain beads
upon my dress
like rotten pearls,
for I brought no cloak
to cover me.
Were I a few years younger
I might consider removing
my dress altogether and running home
in my *camicia,* but that might bring scandal
should it reach the ears of the government,
and I dare not cause my family
embarrassment or punishment.

Carlotta gasps to see me.
"Maria, your mother!"

"Please help me remove
this dress before I do any more harm."

Laughter boils behind me
like hot oil hissing from an open pot.
"What about your fitting, dear sister?
How shall you wiggle your way
clear of that? How could Father
imagine you to be a lady?"

"Do my ears mistake me
or is my sister actually speaking to me?"
The char in my words
stops her clever smile midway.

"What do I care, Maria?"
Vanna squints.
"But Mother will know
you have been out of the house."

This I know, but does my sister
need to keep tally on all I do wrong?
Has she nothing else to do?

FLOODING

The rain prevents travel
across the canal.
It cries down
upon the earth
with anger and passion.
Our furnace floods,
and everyone except me
is called to bail it
and preserve the fires and wood
so we will not lose precious time
we need to produce our glass.

Our palazzo echoes
like an empty drum,
gray and gloomy
as my disposition.
I almost wish to have
been in trouble over my dress
rather than tread water
in my isolated loneliness.

Thunder announces itself,
and a voice calls,
"Hello?"

"No one is here but me, Maria,"
I yell, and scurry to the front hall.

Luca's hair drips a puddle
onto the floor. He slicks it back
with his hand, and his eyes
nearly shimmer silver in the half-light.
"Fetch your cloak. We must go
and move the supplies in the studio."

"But Mother said I was to—"

"Hurry! The rain does not wait
for you to make debate."

I speed up the stairs,
whirl on my cloak
as though it were a cape.

I grasp Luca's hand
and rush into the downpour.
A quiver radiates up my spine.
I quickly release my hold.
"Follow me," I say,
trying to sound authoritative.

OUT OF HARM'S WAY

We lift the soda ash
and the manganese
onto the higher tables.

My cloak feels boulder weight
with rain and cold;
I shake it out in the corner
of the room.

"The rain rages still.
Let's wait here
until she calms a bit."

I nod, though I should return home,
for the studio is drafty,
but mainly it is strange
to be alone with Luca again.

A pregnant silence presides over the room.

"So your father was a master gaffer?"

"No," Luca says.

"Your grandfather?" I ask.

He shakes his head.

"Uncle?" Again I receive a negative response.
"Well, then who?"

"You must delight in your own speech."
Luca smiles at me.

I fold my arms and turn from him.
The mud on my shoes holds more interest.

"I have no family I know of. An old maestro
I swept floors for as a child apprenticed me.
But what does it matter?"

"It doesn't," I say, but I cannot look
at him for fear I might reveal otherwise.

"Well, the rain stopped her throttle,
so we should go back," Luca says.

I nod, for unlike Luca,
soon enough my family
will note that I am gone
and worry where I am.

CALLED TO DUTY

The flood fragmented,
like shells upon the shore,
a whole shipment
of orders Paolo and Luca
labored two weeks
with many apprentices
to prepare.

Even I am called
to staff the ship
and create a batch.
I smile as I dust off
our recipe book.
*Father, steer my rusty
hands with your gentle sail.*

I carry the mixture
down to the furnace.
Luca works inside alone.

I hesitate like a frightened bird,
circle and toe the ground
before I approach him.

"Where is your fancy gown?
Am I not worthy of your finery today?"
Luca's smile is nearly a smirk.

"I might toss this batch
at your head, sir, were it not
three days in the making,"
I say, and set down my bucket.

"You have prepared this.
I thought your full occupation

was feathered caps and wooden shoes."
He laughs. "What kind of glass
shall this mixture produce?"

"You know less than a flea."
I turn to leave.

Luca grabs my arm. "I jest with you.
Please stay and watch a moment
if you like, and we'll see together
what appears."

"And if I don't?"
I say under my breath,
but I sit down.

THE ART OF GLASSBLOWING

The magic of glass
resides in alchemy,
the correct mixture
and preparation
turning stone, ash, metal,
fire, and breath
into clear solid beauty.

The craft of glass
relies less on tools
of the bench
and more on training
the mouth and lips
of the gaffer himself,
the one whose
breath molds the cup
or the vase.

The art of glass
is not color or clarity
or shape alone.
Art births from the mind.
Father always said
a true artist sees
each piece as unique,
as an individual.

Luca preheats the blowpipe
in the furnace's hottest chamber,
then gathers the molten moile
like honey on a dipper.
He rolls his gooey tube,
glowing like a spark turning to flame
on the marble marver's flat surface,
before he dares bring the pipe

to his lips
and blow a bubble
of bright orange-yellow
trimmed in red,
which balloons on the edge
of his tube.
Luca swings round his punty
to his bench and light streams
behind him as if he were an angel.
His jack, blocks, tweezers, paddle,
and shears surround him,
but he reaches for no tool.

He closes his eyes
and imagines the pitcher
in perfect clarity.

It is as though I meet him
for the first time
as he begins to create
his glass art,
and he looks at me
and says,
"The batch is perfect, Maria."

FAMILY SERVICE

Mother examines the sleeve
of my new gown.
"You missed some dirt right here."
Her eyebrow rises like a shadow.
"Remind me again why
you were caught out of doors?"

"I thought I heard Paolo call
for help during the flood rain."

Vanna's mouth opens, her tongue
unfurling like a snail popping
out of its shell, but she says nothing.

"Still, stain or not, this is the latest
fashion, and you should wear it
when you meet the next suitor."

"I thought perhaps Uncle and Marino
would meet with him instead."

"There is far too much work
to do because of the flood.
Besides, I am not sure they
are well equipped to choose
a partner for you," Mother says,
as she untangles my hairpiece.
"This is dreadful."

I nod. "What more can I do to help?"

"Why, Maria, wonderful that you
should ask. Why don't you
take this hair and reweave it?"

I sink as lead in water.
I hoped Mother would let me
continue to help with the batches.
I accept the hairpiece
with a half smile.
"I'll set right to work."

AT SUPPER

I don't care much
for the pot that Carlotta prepares,
but Uncle Giova feasts upon the bones.

"Have you been away at sea?
A starving sailor might eat less than you."
Marino pokes at Uncle.

Uncle laughs as he licks his bone.
"A healthy appetite is good for the soul,
dear nephew."

Mother motions for me to sit more erect
in my chair. I expect Vanna to snicker
as a snorting pig, but she just demonstrates
what Mother meant by "erect"
when Mother's eyes are averted,
just like the old Vanna would have.

Paolo sneezes and we all say,
"May the spirits be blown away,"
because that is what Father always said
whenever someone sneezed.

Luca seems puzzled or maybe
just left out,
like a child without playmates
watching other children
toss around a ball.

Uncle's tone switches from jovial
to officious, from golden hues to ash.
"Seems you had a fine day, Luca?"

"I finished your cups,
if that is what you mean."
Luca does not look up from his bowl.

"All of the old orders from London
are completed?"
Uncle Giova sets down his bone.

Luca nods as he twirls on his cloak.
"Thank you for the meal,"
he says to Mother.

As soon as the door clangs closed,
Mother covers her mouth with her hand.
"Well, how impertinent not to remain
until we are finished. Where did he need
to fly in such haste?"

Paolo crosses to the window.
"He returns to the furnace.
I suppose we are just not fit
to dine with Signore Luca,
not being from the papal line."

Everyone laughs except for me.
But I wonder if perhaps Luca strays
from our family table
for reasons we Baroviers
are too fortunate to understand.

SUNLIGHT

1

When Luca fails to appear
the next morning for our earliest meal,
I hide bread and pears beneath my skirt.
How I will sneak the food
to Luca, I know not.

Mother pulls at her fingers
as though she would pluck
them from her hands
like garden weeds.
She eats not a thing,
which signals Vanna and me
to hurry into our day.

I ask, "Mother, might I practice
walking outside in my new high shoes?"
I expect her to forbid me.

But Mother waves a gesture
of indifference, her mind
sailing on some distant sea.

After Paolo and Marino and Vanna
set to the fornica I slip down the stairs,
my shoes in hand so I make not a clack.
Mother and Uncle pace the parlor.

I feel like a house rat
creeping along the wall
so as not to be caught or trapped.

"He works today cleaning
and preparing the second fornica?"
Mother begs with her wide eyes
to be contradicted.

"We made a contract,
and Luca has the day
to do as he pleases."
Uncle Giova covers Mother's
fluttering hands.

2

Outside, the sun warms my head.
And like a flower opening
its bloom after rain,
I cannot contain my smile.
I stare at the furnace door,
debate knocking,
then call out, "Luca?"
No one answers
so I creak into the cave
of the second fornica.

Cobwebs, dust,
and an overall dank odor
permeate the room.
My eyes adjust to the shadows,
and I discover Luca slumped
in a corner, his eyes shut.

I tap his shoulder,
and he sprouts awake.

"Maria, what are you—?
Could they not afford to buy you
a complete dress?
This one seems not to cover your chest."

I launch the breakfast
I saved for him into his lap.
"It is the latest style."
I feel heated even in the colder room

and fear a flush paints my cheeks.
I cover my face with my hands.

He bites into a pear.
"Thank you. I am famished.
There is more work here
to be done than I supposed."

"I could help you."
The words dribble from my lips
before I consider how
I might be able to do so.

"It is probably better that you don't."

A pang of anger stirred with pain
clamps my center.

He continues, "But if you should visit,
I would always welcome you in."

Luca's eyes stun me.
I can neither move nor speak,
like one under a spell.

I finally nod.
A sticky web caps my hair.
My mouth tastes woolen,
and I cannot think what to say.
I open the door and half stumble
into the street.

3

I smile,
as ornate and obvious in my good cheer
as a jeweled and feathered hat.

Vanna nearly knocks me over
in the street.
She shakes her head.
"Where have you been?"

Even she cannot
vanquish my joy.
"Practicing my walk
in these high shoes," I say.
"And it is a lovely day."

"You hide the truth."
Giovanna pulls a cobweb
out of my hair.
"I saw you come out
of the second furnace.
What were you doing there?"

My smile trampled, I turn to silence,
that great stone wall bricked
between me and my sister.

But Vanna smiles kindly at me.
"Be careful," she says,
and she tucks a loose tendril
behind my ear.

I nod, though my face
must look bewildered
as a beached whale.
Has my sister
decided to return
and the devil
who replaced her
begun to take leave?

ALONE AT LAST

I slide from beneath my mattress
my hidden sketchbook,
and as if possessed
my hand dashes across the paper
until what emerges
from the swirls of chalk
is Luca's face.
His eyes like perfect glass
reflect light off the page.

What surprises me most
is that I draw him in a furnace
I have never visited.
A room buzzing with apprentices
where Luca aids an old man.
Luca is a child, an orphan
whose plight I do not know,
but my mind's eye
envisions the scene complete
and precise.

BY ANY MEANS?

Mother and Uncle and Marino
pile so many orders
upon Luca's back
that he cannot leave
the main fornica to eat,
scarce restore the second one.

I flurry and pace before my window,
a winged dove
trapped behind a glass pane.
Paolo leaves the furnace
with a cartload of beakers,
and I must find a way
to dodge Mother and Vanna.
If only I could fly
or scale the wall.
I hitch one leg up
onto the window's ledge
but then pull it back.

"Why are you spying on Luca?"
Vanna startles me.
I did not notice she had entered the room.

My heartbeat runs like horse hooves,
and again I feel hot.
I say, "I believe there is something
about Luca I must discover."

"Yes, something you must discover
about Luca," Vanna says
with an odd wink.
"Sneak out the servants' door,
and I shall tell Mother
you are resting."

I should not go,
misleading Vanna so,
but I stumble into my shoes
and out the door.

LUCA, ARTIST IN RESIDENCE

Luca is at work when I enter.
I settle myself into a corner
of the room.

I wish to have my sketchbook tonight,
for Luca magics into being
three crystal platters for the Doge's palace,
each more radiant than the last.

Watching him reminds me
of observing my father
as he perfected a new recipe
to make our glass flawless.
A tear brims my eye to think of my father.
I can only imagine
what ache Luca must feel,
never even knowing
his own family.

Luca says nothing to me,
but I know he knows
I have come,
and I know
he is glad that I am here.

QUIET MADNESS

I rustle Vanna from sleep.
"Did Mother come check on me?"

"Yes, but not to worry.
I told her you were resting.
A new suitor visits tomorrow.
I have laid out your dress
and fixed your hairpiece."
Vanna's eyes spider red,
and her face blanches with exhaust.

"But you have so much work
of your own."
I kiss her hands.

Vanna rises upon her elbows,
suddenly more alert.
"Just tell me the truth
about Luca."

"What do you—"

She clasps my hands.
"How do you feel about him?"

I am grateful the night shields
my lying eyes.
"He is a very good gaffer,
and I feel sorry for all
the work he has to do
because of the flood," I say,
and throw my blanket
around myself.

I wish I could trust Vanna.
But even then, what would I tell her—
that when I am with Luca
I long to be molten moile upon his punty,
something he turns to beauty,
a work of art he prizes above all else?
I could not even say this
to the sister I knew before.
It sounds like madness.
And it would likely cause
my family unrest
were I to tangle myself up
with Luca.

"I was wrong, then,"
Giovanna sighs,
and within minutes
I hear the small popping blows
of her sleeping breath.

FULL OF FEATHERS, SHORT OF HAIR

Another old stuffed shirt
Mother and I greet
in the parlor,
aged to be my father
not my husband.
An odd, pudgy man,
why does he not cover
his skull, as he is bald
in the center of his head?
He catches me staring
at his gleaming scalp
bordered by tufts of hair
like sad patches of wiry weeds.
Signore Borosini runs frantic strokes
over and over the top of his head
as if he were polishing it.
I smile at him with a wink
so I can swallow my laughter.

Mother's toe taps mine.
The rain rages against our palazzo,
and I realize I have not heard
one bit of this conversation.

Mother says, "Maria is quite
an accomplished sketch artist."
I open my mouth,
anticipating the question
what do I sketch or
will I show him something.

"Oh." Signore Borosini clears his throat.
"Well, in the shipbuilding business
these days one must be weary
of all suppliers as I am sure

your son, Marino, must have eyes
on his trading partners as well.
Venice is collapsing. After the fall
of Constantinople—doom, doom,
I tell you . . ." And the negative stream
of words about my beloved Murano
and her mother, Venice, never ceases.

I want to scream,
"I will never marry you!"
But I cannot.
I smile politely and say,
"I feel poorly. Please excuse me."
I curtsy and offer my hand to Signore Borosini.
I look him in the eyes,
not at his head.
"Pleasure to meet you. *Buon giorno, signore.*"

Mother could melt glass,
she is so fire-mad at me.
I have never before
left ahead of the suitor.
Mother's eyes flare
their deepest green,
but I surmise
that her anger fuels partially
because she does not want to be
alone with Borosini,
and I have abandoned her.

FOUND GLASS

Giovanna kneels beside my bed,
her head curled over in prayer.
Faceup on my pillow
nestles the hand mirror
Father gave to her
with the larks engraved
on the handle.

"Maria." She startles like doves
being roused. "I did not hear you come in."
Still kneeling, she grasps my hand.
"I have been ugly as an asp.
Please forgive me.
I want to make it up to you."
She offers me her mirror.

"But Father gave this to you," I say.

"Indeed." Vanna nods.
"And I thought it was because
he thought my gifts were limited.
And that is why I have been
so selfish and mean, because
I felt like the only thing I could offer
this family was to marry a nobleman,
whereas you . . ."

"But that is foolish, Vanna," I say.

"Is it? I am not an artist.
But today, I found this mirror,
and instead of it reflecting an image
of myself, it showed our room,
the beauty of our room.
I held the mirror outside,

and how the fornica glimmered.
I want to make things and people
feel beautiful, that is my gift.
I want to help you, Maria.
If you will let me help you,
I know that I can. With your talent
and my assistance, no nobleman
will be able to resist Maria Barovier."

I have never seen my sister's eyes
flutter so rapidly.
It is as though
her lashes are wings.
Her tongue flies from word
to idea like when she sings.

I nod.
"If this will make you happy."

She claps her hands.
"Together we can do this!
I will take great delight in helping
you make a good match.
Mother will be so happy."
Vanna bounds from the room to tell her.

LADY LESSONS

"Hold your shoulders more erect,
chin up, eyes not on the floor
like you are surveying everyone's boots.
It demands then that people
look up to you."
Giovanna's voice is pitched sweeter,
but her words sound
just like Mother's.

Vanna glides across the room,
dancing in her walk.
I try to mimic her steps.
But as if I wear
shoes too large,
I stumble and nearly trip
upon my skirts.

"You looked down, Maria.
That is why you nearly fell."

"But if I don't watch
where I step,
I will certainly break my leg."

"Use your hips and arms
to balance, and hold
your center tight."

"Oh, I give up.
Please, Vanna, I need a rest.
Let me take off this dress and shoes.
Could I not sneak
down to the furnace
and see if I might discover
something of Luca?"

Vanna aids me out of my finery.
"Why would you care to do that?"

I should tell her, but instead I say,
"I don't know. Just . . ."
My voice breaks.
"I must go."

And I whip down the stairs
faster than any noblewoman
should dare to go.

I AM HERE

I don't even want to speak
to him today.
All he needs to do
is turn back
from the radiance
of the furnace
all silhouetted bronze
and ember glow
and acknowledge
that I am here.

Luca notes my presence
and tosses me an apron.
"What, have you come
to just look and stare, princess?
Or might you not lend a hand?"

FAILING

Mother wraps prayer beads
round her wrists.
She has just come from cathedral
and calls me into her chambers.
I kneel before her.

She finally speaks to me.
"I have been praying
over what to do with you, Maria.
You left a meeting with a suitor
without my consent."

"I am sorry. I don't know what—"

She raises her hand
like a shield and silences my words.

Tears trickle down her cheeks.
"You take none of this seriously.
I am failing you as a mother,
but worse I am failing your father."

She dries her eyes.
"If you cannot make a match
with Signore Bembo,
I may have to send you to the convent."

MY SISTER, MY CAPTAIN

Giovanna hums softly a tune
that sounds smooth and pleasant
as golden brocade.
I wish for it never to end.

"I know a little of Signore Bembo;
he is related to the Doge.
An older man who should have
married long ago and is a bit
of an embarrassment to his family,
and that is why we have a chance
to make this alliance,"
she says after morning meal.
"I have met his sister.
She is odd, wears her hair
plaited three ways and very tightly.
And she speaks
out of the side of her mouth,
but her brother adores her."
Vanna cannot even drink her coffee
she is so eager to prepare
for our suitor.
She says nothing about
my running off
to see Luca.

She flings open my bureau
with such force I fear
the door will unhinge.
Vanna paces before
the open closet, contemplating
what I should wear as though
this were of vital import.
It is as though she prepares

me for battle. Finally selecting
the green silken frock, she says,
"This is the gown that will snare
Signore Bembo." Her eyes ignite.

"Vanna, you take this so seriously,"
I say.

"Maria, this man will acquire
great wealth from our family.
You do not realize your worth," she says.
"Of course, the Bembos
are a very political family
in Venice and well aligned for us.
That is why it is a good match."

"I had no idea you knew
so much of this," I say.

"When you spent time learning recipes
with Father, what do you suppose
Mother and I did, solely pull
thread through tapestry?
No, I learned the history
of certain families of which
I might become a part."

"Why did Mother not tell me
these things to help me understand?"
I ask her.

Vanna shrugs. "Perhaps
there wasn't time
or she assumed that I would help you.
I have failed you to this point,
but no more."

My sister stands up taller
than I have ever seen her.
"Andrea Bembo,
if I recall correctly, likes figs.
His sister, Leona, likes gardens.
You should draw a picture
of a garden for her."

Vanna lists items like a captain.
I rush about the room,
a mad puppy trailing
her skirt tails,
trying to take notes
and complete tasks.
But I fear we have not
enough time
and that my heart—
I certainly haven't time
to consider that.

DOWRY

I hold the will
but must misread what it says.
Vanna's words were truth.
My dowry alone
could restore both fornicas.

"What are you doing rifling
through your father's papers?"
Mother grabs the will
from my hands.

"I don't need all of these ducats
for my dowry.
Why don't you use them
for the business?"

"Maria, I cannot just reallocate
funds from a will as I see fit.
Only you can give money back
to this family from your dowry,
and only upon your death.
And I wish that to happen no time soon."
Mother shakes her head.
"This was never to be your concern."

"But why not?
Perhaps if you had told me
all that was at stake,
I might have been more helpful."

Mother puts her arms around me.
"Oh, my dear, a mother knows
her children, and I am not sure
that you can be any more

than you are. I wish you
had never found this."

"But now I know
I cannot disappoint you," I say.

Mother just shakes her head.

THE QUESTION I AM NOT SUPPOSED TO ASK

We are tucked in our beds.
The night's faintest stars
glitter through the window
like crystal lace.
"Vanna?" I whisper her name,
uncertain whether I wish her
asleep or awake.

"Yes?"

"I know this sounds selfish,
but what about love and happiness?
Am I even to consider that?"

"I knew you would ask this, Maria."
Her voice smiles at me even
through the dark. "Mother
said that comes later."

"But how?" I ask. "I mean what if—"

"I don't know everything, Maria,"
Vanna says, a twang of annoyance
in her tone. "Andrea Bembo
is said to have many charms.
You will have to discover yourself
what delights you about him."

But that was not what I meant
at all.

SIGNORE BEMBO

When I see him my legs fall limp
and I almost timber under my skirt.
Giovanna described the man
as distinguished and charming,
but he seems to be another bald man
with sad squinty eyes.

I straighten my posture
and paint on a smile.
And remember this is not about me.

Mother asks, "How was your travel
to Murano?"

"Very well," he says. Andrea Bembo's
face opens and closes like a clamshell
but does not change shape when he speaks.
He is the color of putty.
My sons will look like mud.

"Maria has prepared a sketch
for your sister, Leona."
Mother urges me to present
it to him.

Andrea smiles at my drawing
of our backyard garden in bloom.
My favorite part is the sand martin
trapped behind the glass window.
He accepts the sketch graciously.
"Leona will like this.
We both appreciate fine art. *Grazie.*"

I nod and smile
at his kind words,

though I wish to run.
I feel like something
is being decided upon
here and now
that is beyond anyone's choice.

FLORAL DELIVERY

Ranunculus arrive
by the basketful
in vibrant reds and yellows
and fuchsias,
all telling me that
Andrea Bembo finds me
"radiant with charms."

Mother's face turns
to summer sun.
Giovanna clasps her hands.
"Well done, Maria!
He must have liked
the sketch and the dress
and you."

I feed off of their excitement
like a nursing child.
I am so happy to please them.

The flowers smell fresh
and successful.

DAY AND NIGHT

The preparation
to be ready for
the ceremonies of preparation
I am not prepared for.
For now, we are to keep
the news of our plans
to be betrothed secret,
but we prepare nonetheless.
Noble girls begin learning these rituals
of dance and dress and dining and etiquette
when they begin breathing.
I cannot even stand properly
in the garments. And it seems I will need
more fine garments to be wed
than my family has possessed altogether
in my entire fifteen years of living.
I am covered in pinpricks
and stand nearly twelve hours
to be fitted by tailors;
all the while Vanna rattles
my ears, naming the five hundred guests
who will attend my banquets,
people I have never heard of,
no one from Murano.
And I must be able to greet them all,
but especially know the relations
between all the ducal family.

"For after the ship
takes you to consummate your marriage
and live in the house
of Andrea Bembo and his father,
you shall not return to us"—
Vanna can hardly
finish the last words—

"but only wave us good-bye
from on board."

The tears stream my face.
"Surely that cannot be
the tradition."

"No, you belong to them."

"I must be alone."
I usher everyone, even Vanna,
out of my room.

The moon crests low in the sky
tonight. I ignore my call to dine.

Comfort comes only one way—
when I stare at the second fornica
and imagine myself inside its warmth,
then pick up my chalk.
My sketchbook fills with pictures.
Like a carafe overfilling with water,
like a garden blooming boatloads
of flowers, I cannot contain
the images in my head.
And all of them Luca.

REPLENISHMENT

Instead of breakfast
I sneak out the servants' door.

In the smolder of the furnace Luca shines.

"What would you do
if you could not blow glass?"
I ask him.

He lowers his blowpipe.
"I have never considered it.
To make glass to me at this point
is to breathe. Whatever else I did
would be inconsequential."

"Father always said he would have been
as a sailor adrift, without compass or stars—
a blind sailor," I say.

"It is as if you know my mind."
Luca twirls the pipe to cool down
his glass, but his focus is all on me.
"Do you blow glass, Maria?"

"No. I might try it someday,
but Father never permitted me."
I look at him straight, not lowering
my eyes. "But I do sketch."

"Show me sometime."

I nod agreement,
but what will I show him
when all I render lately
is Luca himself?

A SECOND SISTER

A boat of grandeur
filled with fruits and flowers
awaits Mother and Vanna and me
at Murano's main harbor.

Andrea sent it for us
so that we can visit his sister, Leona,
today. As I step aboard,
I tremble, for I leave my island
for the first time.
With each pull of the ferryman's oar,
Murano quickly diminishes behind us
until it seems my home has been
swallowed by the sea.
Vanna looks not at all behind her
but only forward onto Venice.

Venice towers, all the buildings
double or triple the size of those
on Murano. As they lift me off the boat,
I fear I will fall into the canal
and disappear like my island behind me.

We board a gondola
to the Palazzo Bembo
where Leona awaits us.
"There is the Ducal Palace
and Piazza San Marco."
Vanna points out these places
as if they were as familiar to her
as the fornicas at home.

The sun so bright I squint,
all I can see is swirls of color,
a smeared canvas.

I clutch the boat's rail.
My breath puffs and puffs.
I should be delighting in the architecture
of this new scenery, but I feel
like my father's blind sailor here,
as if I am drowning.

"Maria, you look faint, child,"
Mother says. "Perk up now."
And then I see it,
a smudge at first,
but then aside the great Rialto Bridge
sits a palazzo that could feast upon
and hold three of our little palazzi
inside its belly, it is that grand.
A girl stands so still and strict
I think at first she must be stone,
but then I see she has Andrea's unblinking eyes.
No smile crosses Leona's lips
as I come into view.
She waves to Vanna,
but I receive a dead stare,
and then Leona shows me
the back of her hat.

She can show me her hat
as much she desires now,
but once I live in that palazzo,
like it or not, she will have
to face my face.

ANDREA'S SURPRISE

The palazzo will devour me,
I am sure of it.
Three servants wait
on each of us, one with wine,
one with water,
one with capon?

How did they know
my favorite dish?
"Mother, did you tell
them what to serve?"
I try to make my voice
a whisper, but Leona overhears.

"My dear, naive Maria,
did you not think
Andrea would provide
you what you like to eat?"
Her tone swats at me like a fly.

I am about to shove
the veal-stuffed sausage
up her veal-stuffed nose
when Vanna says,
"It was very considerate of Andrea."

"My brother is a delight,"
Leona says.

I can't be sure I agree,
but before I have time
to weigh the evidence

my sister says,
"Maria, it is a lovely frame
they have chosen, is it not?"
Vanna points to the wall.

My sketch of the garden hangs,
my first ever mounted,
and right beside a Bellini.
I almost want to dance,
but it would be most improper,
and mostly I fear
it might allow Leona
some sort of satisfaction.

Leona says,
"Yes, Andrea chose the frame.
Lovely, isn't it?"

And I do agree, but for now
I keep it to myself.

DIVIDED

The waves lash
against the ferry
and we are beat to and fro
in the sea, sometimes pushed
toward Murano and sometimes
toward Venice.

The sun sets and all blazes,
so that I cannot distinguish
which island is home.

Would it not have been easier
if Andrea had been a clod?
But part of me is somewhat drawn
to Venice, her grandeur
and estate. And Andrea
made me feel welcome,
even if his sister did not.

A NEW SUBJECT

Now more than ever I must show Luca
the work of my hands,
of my head, the pictures that flow
and bubble from inside of me,
but my fingers shake to sketch
anything today.

Suddenly my hand slicks across the page
like a bird in pursuit darts the sky.
I close my eyes and outline her face
and hair. I open my eyes to capture
the way Vanna sees beyond the window.
I remember the wonder with which
she beheld Venice and draw it into
Vanna's smile.

Later when we discuss
the wedding preparations
and plan another voyage to Venice
and the Bembo palazzo, I do not grit
my teeth but instead study my sister.
I will memorize her face and the setting
around her, the gardens, the tables,
paintings, and cloths. I will sketch
this all for Luca. I will find less horror
now in traveling across the sea,
less discomfort in my shoes.
I will focus and not speak
out of turn, just capture the scene
for my canvas
and show it all, one day soon,
to my dear gaffer.

CREATION

I sneak down to the fornica.
Luca smiles as though
I had let the entire sun
into the room.

"What are you working on today?"
I ask him.

"I am not working right now,
but hush and do not tell your
uncle and brothers."

"Dear Luca, I hate to tell you,
but there is something forming
out of the moile on your punty."

"I know this, but when one
loves what he does as much
as I do, can it be called work?"
he says with a wink.

I want to throw my apron
at Luca then, but I understand
what he means.
"Creation can be a gift."

"You are a very smart girl, Maria."

APPRECIATION

Mother leaves me to sit
alone with Andrea,
my soon-to-be betrothed,
and I tug at my sleeve for lack
of what to say or do.

Vanna would be full
of topics. I force an awkward smile
and say,
"It is a beautiful day."

"Yes, the sea appears to melt
into the sky this morning."

Andrea's words surprise me.

"My uncle says it is always
days like this that promise
to bring darkest rain clouds
by afternoon." I want to stuff
my sleeve down my throat.
Can I speak of nothing but weather?

"Well, Ovid said,
'Beauty is a fragile gift.'
Guess we best enjoy
the day while we can.
Shall we stroll the garden?"

Andrea takes my arm
and for once I feel
like a true lady,
the way I imagine
Vanna must feel
on most days.
And it is nice.

TWO SUITABLE SUITORS?

How is a girl to choose
between a green dress
and a blue?

One pleases your family,
the other pleases you.

One man appreciates beauty,
is kind, and fulfills your duty.

The other creates glass,
but what of the future if he knows no past?

To follow the head
or the heart,
this is the question
that rips me apart.

THE SKETCHBOOK

As soon as Vanna and Mother
set to the market,
when I am to study
the ducal lineage
alone in my chambers,
I hide the sketchbook
under my skirt and slip
out of my bedroom.

He doesn't notice me at first.
And there is a moment
when I nearly turn to run.
It is as though all
motion stops like the stillness
right before
the howl of a rainstorm.
I feel as though
I could dash and escape,
as if underneath my feet
a path emerges wherein
I could leap
one way to the door
or the other toward Luca.
While I hesitate,
Luca turns round.
"Is that your sketchbook?"

I must then bring it forth.
My steps wobble
and he pries
the book from my clutch.

I retreat to the shadows
like a cockroach
scared of light.

Luca turns the pages slowly.
I have brought him only five drawings
from my new book.
He waves me over.

"This is your sister, no?
I never realized how beautiful
she is." Luca's eyes radiate in a way
I have never seen.
He breathes in deeply
as if to inhale the drawing.
Of course, he is looking at Vanna—
the curve of her face.
He cannot quite speak now,
all that emerges from his lips
is *"Bella,"* and his eyes, his silly
sparkling eyes, they never lift from the page.

MI DISPIACE (I'M SORRY)

I snatch back the sketchbook and run.
I might have left black marks
upon the floor, I exited so quickly.
I will not permit Luca the satisfaction
of my foolish brimming eyes.
What did I expect, everyone loves Vanna.
In my stomach a black crow
caws its wicked claws out for sisterly
vengeance, but before I reach
our chambers the crow has been
digested. It is not Vanna's fault
that Luca prefers her. She did not even
ask me to draw a sketch of her.
Her beauty is crystal,
and I am clay.

The foolishness is all my own
for even thinking he would ever care for me.
I know now why Father
willed me to a senator;
no one else
would have me.

"Maria!" The voice nets me like a fish.

I hide no tears from Mother.

"What is in your hands?"

I give up the sketchbook.
I give it all up.
I tell her about my visits
to see Luca
and my foolish feelings for him.

I kneel beside her
and clutch her legs
and let the tears torrent
and the apologies stream
out of my unclogged mouth.

Mother listens with no scolding.
She cradles my head
and wipes my tears
with her thumb.
Though I am crumbling
Mother's arms form
a moat around me.

"Mother, please don't tell anyone
about my feelings for Luca."

"Of course not, sweet Maria."

She leafs through my sketchbook
and brushes off the drawings of Vanna.
"These are quite lovely, Maria.
I see why Luca admired them so."

"You can burn them if you like.
I will pray a thousand prayer beads
for disobeying you."

"No, my dear.
I think you have been clever
without realizing it.
You may have solved
a great problem for your family,
Maria. Perhaps Luca's fondness
for Giovanna will prove
to be good *and* profitable."

NO CHOICE

There is no choice
to make,
and I should rejoice
that I am no longer
torn between the shores
of Murano and Venice,
but somehow it only
makes the sorrow
of leaving my glass home
more great.

I SPY

On our next trip
to the Bembo palazzo
we are led into a great hall.
Portraits and paintings line
the walls. A floor-to-ceiling tapestry
finer than I have ever laid eyes upon
captures the great Venetian victories.
I say to Leona, "You sew very well,"
and point at the grand tapestry.

She eyes me like a peasant child.
"The servants do that work,
instructed by commissioned artists."

When Leona spins her back to us,
Vanna just places a finger to her lips,
indicating it would be best I keep silent.

Vanna says, "Leona, I noticed
when we walked through the arbor
how your peonies flourish."

Leona smiles for the first time,
and she is actually quite pretty.
"Yes, the French peonies have been
most magnificent this season."

I was not sure which one was a peony.
Leona's garden must contain a thousand
varieties of flowers and all of them gorgeous.
I hear a small rumble behind me
like a little mouse, and I smile for the first time.
So the Bembos are not perfect;
they too have rodents in the parlor.

I investigate further
as we are called to tea
and discover
a pair of very recognizable
boots and two peeping eyes.
The calamity I heard
was no mouse
but belongs to none other
than the man to whom I will be
betrothed, Andrea Bembo.
He half hides behind drapery
and spies upon us ladies.

I find this rather odd,
as Andrea has been most distinguished
up to this point.
But while
Mother and Vanna and Leona
discuss fashion and the marriage
preparations, I just watch to see
if Andrea will stumble and be discovered.
He manages to stay rather well concealed
to the others.

Andrea watches the other ladies
but notes not that I scout him.
I scoot my chair closer
to the window dressing.
He covers himself with it
like a cape, this man
who is twenty years my senior,
as if that will help.
I notice now that his eyes
are upon one particular lady—
Giovanna.
He smiles like a tickled babe.

I know this look well.
It is the look every man
stuns into when he sees and hears Vanna.
I realize slowly
that he has never seen
my sister before.

"Please sing something,"
Leona asks Vanna.

I think I may be sick
directly into my feathered hat,
or worse I may cry.
But Vanna cannot refuse.
And the terrible part
is that Giovanna
remains innocent,
so I cannot be angry at her a smidge.
But I *can* be furious at him,
hideous him, idiot Andrea!

First Luca, now Andrea.
I will have no one,
and Vanna will have them all.
I slump in my chair,
cross my arms over my chest,
kick off my uncomfortable shoes,
and tug at my tightly bound corset—
very unladylike.
Mother nearly growls at me.

And I don't care.

YOU CAN HAVE THAT BUMBLING BEMBO

On the boat ride home
I tell Mother and Vanna
that Andrea was hiding
behind the curtains like a baby,
and they find it charming.

"He adores you so,
he wants to be in your presence,"
Vanna says.

"Whether or not it is appropriate,
it is certainly sweet,"
Mother adds.

"It is stupid. And besides,
he wants to be near Vanna,
you fools. He wants nothing
to do with me. It is like
she charms snakes
with her voice." I begin to hiss.

My cruelty shatters Vanna.
"I have only been trying
to help unite our families.
I never mean to harm
anyone with my singing.
You don't realize how
lucky you are to marry Andrea.
You will have children.
I will have prayer beads, Maria."

My mother can hardly believe
Vanna has said these words aloud,
and neither can I.

But if Mother has her way,
Vanna's words will not be true.

NOWHERE TO GO

This is the lonely place.
The cold stone prison,
windowless and damp,
where I live by myself.
No one understands.

Mother has banished me
to my chambers,
but it matters not.

I cannot retreat
to the warmth of the fornica.
I am not wanted there.

Giovanna has been sent
with the batches instead.

INDISCREET

Carlotta's stew smells rotten
tonight, though I know
it is not.
It is the man seated
at the table's end
who decays in his chair
and stinks up our supper.

"Will you please pass the loaf?"
Luca asks Vanna in a smiling voice,
his cheeks bloated wide as a stuffed fish.

When she gives him the bread,
he holds her hand too long
and looks at her eyes
as though studying her face.
Vanna's neck turns the same
shade of pink as those peonies
she so adored in Leona's garden.

I want to smash my goblet.
I want to harden to glass
and shatter upon the floor.
Does no one else see
this display of indiscretion?

I search the table.
Uncle stuffs his mouth.
Marino reads a pamphlet,
and Paolo distracts himself
with something beyond
the windowpane.

But Mother
grins a wide smile
like a self-satisfied cat
after it snares a rabbit.
Mother has seen what I witnessed,
and she nods
in approval.

MOTHER'S PLAN

Mother calls Giovanna and me
to her chambers.
"As we know, your father decreed
that Maria should marry a nobleman,
and that shall gladly be Signore Bembo,
but your father said nothing of what
was to become of Giovanna."

She motions for us to kneel down
before her as if she were the cardinal.
"I feel it would be a great disservice
to Giovanna and this family to send her
to the convent as is the tradition
in most families. Yet we have not much
to offer in the way of a dowry for Vanna.
One suitor, however, may be willing
to acquire a somewhat unconventional dowry.
And he appears already to fancy you,
Giovanna."

I know what Mother is going to say,
but I clasp my hands to the Virgin Mother
in prayer that Mother's words be pulled back.

"Luca wishes to own the second fornica
outright. He could be given it as a dowry,
and then as he is an orphan
with no living relations to speak of
it would actually remain in our family."

Giovanna's face sinks like silt
to the ocean floor.
"But Mother—"
she begins her protest.

Mother raises her hand.
"No, my mind is firm.
Uncle Giova and your brothers agree."

I barely balance on my knees.
I feel as though my legs will be
swallowed into the floor
surely as my heart.

Mother turns now only to Giovanna.
"We do not propose this plan to Luca yet
but would give him time to grow in fondness
for you, Giovanna. Do you understand?"

Vanna closes her eyes, then tosses back
her mane. I want to rip the golden locks
from her head for the first time.
She nods. "Yes, Mother. I shall do my best."

CONFLICT

"Maria, why do you mope so?"
Vanna fixes me
with a raised eyebrow.
Her hands are dirty
from preparing a batch
to be made into glass,
but still not one of her hairs
falls out of place.
"You were to brush your hair
and put on your blue gown."
She touches my cheek
and I coil away.
"Have you been crying?"

"Oh, bite an asp, Vanna!
What do you know?
I am not going to the Bembo palazzo."

"You are so!" Her pretty little
voice loud as cathedral bells now.

"Why, are you so eager to marry Luca?
Well, it seems you can choose
a husband, dearest sister.
Andrea Bembo or Luca.
Everyone's eyes, all for you."
My voice that began as a storm
siphons down to a trickle
as the tears begin to fall.

Giovanna drapes her arm
over my shoulders, her voice
quiet again. "Sister, you are wrong.
The devil himself
is more correct in his thinking.

Andrea will be your betrothed.
He cannot have eyes for me.
Sometimes . . . Oh, never you mind."

I want to stop sniffling
in front of her,
but I can't.

She exhales with exhaust. "And Luca,
he orders me and demands
pincers and jacks, and the batch
is never pure enough.
He never looks me in the eye.
He has no manners.
It is as if he has surmised Mother's plan
and rebels against it. It is as though
he wishes for me to dislike him.
And then today he asked again
and again after you until I wished
to throw the blocks at him."

I smile. I cannot stop myself.

"This pleases you.
That I am going to fail my family.
You are a funny girl,"
Vanna says, as she helps me into my dress.

A CHANGE IN THE WEATHER

I can barely huff out my sentences.
"I don't want you to fail.
Well, I suppose that I do.
But really it is just
that I don't want you to succeed
with Luca. Did Luca really
ask after me?" I say to Vanna,
and tug at my corset strings.

"I thought that you agreed
to marry Andrea?"
My sister looks at me
as though I am a cloud
obscuring an otherwise blue sky.
"Why are you suddenly going
against the plans?"

Oh, the rains come to my eyes
and rage down upon my face,
and I can't help but blurt it out.
"I think that I . . .
that I, well, I care for Luca."

The clouds have left Vanna's
head. She smiles.
"So now you finally admit
what I knew all along."

I nod and snuffle like a child.

"Well, this is a fine mess,"
she says, and mops the tears
from my dress.

Mother arrives like hail,
unexpected and not at all
what we wanted or needed
in terms of a change of weather.
"Girls, our ship
for the Bembo palazzo
has just arrived."

SORELLA (SISTER)

How am I supposed to act?
Vanna and I did not have
time to formulate a plan.
Mother has her tidy little notions
tucked in like bed linens,
or so she believes,
though I toss and turn
on my mattress and sweat
the sheets in nightmares.

Leona recites for me, without heart,
the names of her aunts. "Lucretia,
Margaretta, Josephine, Rosaria—*ricordare* her,
she is the one with the twin sons,"
she says, as if I will remember
any of this, as if Leona wants
to call me *sorella.*

Then I spy him again behind
a hydrangea bush.
Does Andrea not have
senatorial business to attend to?
I call out, "Andrea,"
as I should not, but I don't care,
he should not scrounge in bushes.

At first Andrea thinks to scamper
away like a rat, but then he brushes
off his vest and approaches us.
"*Buongiorno,*" he says.
He kisses first my mother's hand
and then mine, but finally my sister's.
And it does seem to me that once again
a man grasps Vanna's palm
tighter than he should, and his lips

linger on her fingers a few seconds
longer than is decorous.
Andrea looks up into her eyes,
and Vanna smiles at him
as though Andrea handed her
a thousand ducats, as though
something magical has passed
between them.

"We are planning the seating
arrangements for the betrothal
ceremony and processional."
Leona's lips curl up like a gondola
in the presence of her brother.
She also is taken in by his apparent charm—
a man stumbling from a bush?

They seem a happy family.
And yet somehow when I
step aboard the Bembo boat
it capsizes, as though my weight
upsets its careful balance.

Giovanna shimmers at the Bembo
palazzo. She seems already
to be a sister of Leona's
and sits comfortably at the table
during meal.

"I love the hat you chose
for the betrothal dress, Maria."
Leona points at my head
with a bit of hope.

"Vanna selected it," I say quietly.
I see the gondola sink
deeper into the sea for me

and swing its door wide
for Giovanna.

"I should have surmised," Leona says,
in a voice reserved for children.

Part of me wishes
to thrash my tongue at her.
But I just rap my fingers on my knees,
knowing we soon leave port for Murano.

The noon sun
shines bright and direct upon us.
The glare catches Vanna's eyes
such that she pains, and I remove
my new hat and place it upon
my sister's head.
It looks so lovely, feathered
and correct. It always belonged
upon her crown. And after the
fierce sun passes when Vanna
tries to give it back, I refuse
to take it.

MI RIFIUTO (I REFUSE)

I refuse to accept
that nothing can be done
but to accept
that I must marry Andrea Bembo
and Giovanna must marry Luca.

I refuse to believe
we should follow a will
that breaks tradition and hearts and sense
like a crew who go down
with their sinking vessel
when we all can
kick and swim to shore.

I grab my sketchbook
and rush to the place
I feel most afloat—
the fornica.

BETROTHAL GOBLET

The goblet's beauty terrifies
like a gem so large
it overwhelms the hand
that wears it.

"Well, does the noblewoman
herself come
to examine her wares?"
He bows down
in an exaggerated curtsy
and extends me the glass.
"I present your betrothal goblet."

I wish to hurl it at his face,
but instead I set it upon the table.

Luca and I stare at the azure glass,
yet unadorned. I should like
to smash it to a thousand shards.
A scroll of paper tangles
inside the cup's neck
with flowers and birds
and an inscription
I refuse to accept.

"What is that?"
I point to the paper
in horror.

"The outline for the enameler.
Do you think they just place
glass upon glass without thought—
no, he must know what to paint."

Luca will no longer look at me.
"Well, take your marriage glass."

"I will not," I say.

"Fine, I shall send it with Vanna,
then. What business do you have
in my fornica anyway? Go away,"
he says, with his back turned to me still.

I pick up the ugly scroll
that taints Luca's work
and quietly tuck it into my dress.
"No, I wish to stay," I say,
but my voice is no larger
than a pebble in a child's hand.

VULNERABLE

Luca's back transforms
from a barrier into a shield,
and I ask with a voice
quiet as a spider spinning a web,
"Luca, do you want to marry
Vanna?"

His turn is soft
as though he were on wheels.
"I want to own the second fornica.
I do not hide this from anyone.
And there is nothing
wrong with your sister."

As I step closer
to the fire of the fornica
and Luca,
my shadow lengthens.
"I understand.
And you are correct.
My sister is wonderful."

"What is that you clutch
so tightly?" Luca gestures
to my sketchbook. I almost
forgot that I held it in my arms.

I shake my head no.
Even though I brought it
for him to see,
now I feel I have made
a dreadful mistake.

He wrangles it from my grasp,
and I crumble backward

a few steps like someone
yanked and released my hair.
Luca flips quickly through the sheets.
"But these are all of me?" he says
with that accusing voice of his.

The tears sting, but it is too late
now to run away unknown.
"Yes, you fool, of course they are.
Don't you know?"

I am swift as gale winds
toward the door,
but Luca blocks my way.

"Stay. Sit down.
Listen now to how *I* feel,
sweet Maria."

His hand upon my arm
so warm and gentle,
I melt and bend.
And I know now
he will never allow me
to shatter upon the floor.

LIFTING THE FOG

Luca clasps my hand full
in his and leads me to the bench,
a true gentleman. We sit so close
beside one another our ankles touch,
our hands still laced.

He begins, "I feel as though I have
been in a great fog with you, Maria,
ever since that first moment when
you asked me did I not know
what thyme was."

I smile.

He squeezes my hand.
"The fog has been lovely
and mysterious, and I have enjoyed
treading and searching through it
for you, but now the weather lifts
and you stand before me in all
your light. And I am not sure
that I deserve you,
for I do not know what a family is,
having neither a mother nor a father
to remember."

There is a moment when
I think a tear may form
in the crook of his eye.
I want to kiss all his sadness away,
drown it in an ocean of my cheer,
but Luca continues,
"My heart feels for you
like I feel for my greatest glass,
only more, but I am not certain
that this is enough."

He tries to go on,
but I put a finger to his lips
and draw a smile.
"Oh, but it is," I say.
"It is more than I could dream
to ask for from anyone. I have
even imagined myself your glass,
only until now I believed
my feelings would shatter me.
And even that
didn't stop me caring for you."

Luca kneels before me now.
"Never would I break
one I wish to call family,"
he says.

MY PROTECTOR

Between me and the world,
my sister has always been
safe bedrock in a sinking marsh.

She is a straw hat against noon glare,
a melody bludgeoning night gloom.

Between me and my doubts,
my sister is a shore
that breaks tides apart.
Her cathedral bells ring
day in and out.

Between me and my mother,
my sister is cristallo.
She can see both sides
and remain lovely and unbroken
to each.

Between me and my impatient heart,
my sister navigates breakwaters
with steady hands.

So what if I
have stolen from my sister
a thing she precious desires to keep—
her chance to become a bride?

HOW TO EXPLAIN

Before I can think of what to say
to plea my side of it,
Vanna grasps my hands.

"Maria, I have a solution.
You see, I think I know
how to solve all of these entanglements.
Why are you so flushed
and yet pale? Sit down.
Where have you been?"
My sister's words
are rapid as a hailstorm,
and I think I may faint
if I stay on my feet.

"I was with Luca, and, Vanna, I—"

"Wonderful," Vanna says.
"You must be with him.
Marry him, I mean, for that
is your true destiny.
And I just know
that is what he wishes too.
Sisters know these things."
Vanna cannot stop talking.
It is as though her mouth
spits dragon fire.
"I know this sounds odd to you,
but I think I may wish to marry
Andrea Bembo. I know
that you find him clumsy at times,
but his awkwardness is quite
precisely his charm to me.
And I do believe it is my destiny
to become a Bembo.

So now all we need to do
is to execute a plan."

"Oh, yes," I say with excitement.
"What is the plan?"

"Well, I supposed that you
would think of that portion."
Vanna looks blankly at me
for a moment.
"I jest,"
she finally says.
"I am not certain yet,
but I do know that I must go
directly to visit Leona
and ask for her aid
in this switching of sisters
we propose."

Leona helping me,
well that would be quite
different, but if Vanna
thinks it possible . . .

"You keep Mother occupied,"
Vanna says.

"How am I to do that?"
I ask Giovanna.

"Oh, Maria. Now, you can think
of something you both enjoy,"
Vanna says, and swooshes off
faster than a gale wind.

A LAYER OF ENAMEL

Mother and I polish the beakers,
and she bombards me again
with betrothal ceremony preparations.
"We must think again about
what sort of play act we should hire
to amuse our guests. It is tradition,
of course, to . . ."
Her voice is a stream of babble
I scarce understand and care
less about than boiled cabbage.

"The betrothal goblet that Luca made?"
I ask her.

Mother perks up at the word *betrothal*
from my lips. I so rarely utter it.
"Yes, it certainly is fine," she says.

"How does the enameler inscribe and apply
the decoration to the glass?" I ask her.

Fully deflated by my technical question,
not related in fact to marriage preparations,
Mother demands, "What does it matter, Maria?"

"I just want the glass to be perfect,
as it reflects on Father and our family."

"I had not thought of that."

I ask her again, "Do you know the technique?"

"The enameler in essence paints on the enamel,
which is also glass. I believe then that the goblet
is reheated to a melting point so the enamel

attaches to the goblet but not so severely
that the glass entirely loses its shape.
Why don't you take the goblet
to the enameler and see for yourself?" she says.

"May I?"

"Did I not just give you permission?"

"Mother, I also took liberty to draw
some improved birds and flowers
to adorn the cup and traced them
onto a scroll for the enameler."
I hand my sketchbook
with simple outlines of doves
and roses to Mother.
"Here is the sketch I made,
but I want the final glass to be a present
for Andrea from me and none to see it
beforehand."

"This is a lovely gesture," she says,
and launches back into talk of the ceremony,
what we shall eat, where I shall sit,
what everyone shall wear,
her words as dull as
the unpolished glassware before us.

But right now I could run barefoot
on broken cullet I am so pleased.
For the first portion of my plan
seems to be set.

ENAMELER

Gold is leaf-cut, pressed,
and then fixed into place
with a gummy mixture
just as bricks are laid upon each other
and set to dry in the sun.
The gilder scrapes away
the hearts I marked along the lip
of the betrothal goblet
as carefully as he shaves
hair from his chin.
The enamel is then painted
along my tracings with a fine brush—
first a blue glass paste, then crimson,
then green. The scene
of two lovers exchanging rings,
each astride a horse,
comes to life.

The woman shakes
out bejeweled blond locks,
which none can mistake.
They belong only to one girl,
my sister, Giovanna.
And the man
with the family crest Bembo
can be none other than Andrea.

The cup dries
and heats inside
the annealer so glass
fuses to glass—
and my design
is forever captured
upon Luca's work.

MY OWN PLAN

My plan is
to ask Andrea
to marry my sister,
no, to ask Andrea
to ask my sister to marry him,
no, to ask Andrea if he wants
to ask my sister if she wants
to marry him.

My plan is
more complicated
than I thought.

My plan begins
with a boat
and a prayer
and a trip to visit Luca.

DISHONOR

As I enter the fornica
I can hardly believe my eyes.
Luca and *Andrea*?

Andrea draws his sword on Luca.
"I should report you
to the Council of Ten
or slay you here now
for trying to take Maria
from me when she and I have
signed a contract to be ringed.
I would be just to do so."

"True enough." Luca sets down
his blowpipe, his arms free
and wide in surrender.

I want to rush between them,
to yank the hem of Andrea's shirt
like a child tugs her mother's skirt
for attention. I want to hold Andrea
and his weapon back
from moving toward Luca.
But all I can do is remain
where I stand. Andrea must
have found out about me and Luca
from my sister and Leona.
And he either does not want
to marry my sister
or cannot.

The sword tip grazes
Luca's blouse. I never
realized the sinister angle
of Andrea's nose, the strength

and cruelty of his shoulder blade.
"You dishonor my family,
Luca—" and Andrea
pauses thirty-three measures
to think of Luca's given name.
"What is your family name?"
Andrea asks,
momentarily lowering his sword.

"I have none, sir.
Or do not know what it is."
Luca stares at Andrea with those eyes
that turn cullet to molten glass.
I wonder what, if any, effect
they might cause upon Andrea.

"Curious," Andrea says,
again brandishing his weapon.

And then a small tumble
of jacks, blocks, and pincers
turns my head, and Vanna cries,
"No, please, Andrea, stop!"
Andrea's expression melts
from madness to near joy
at the sight of my sister.

SWAP

Leona follows my sister
into our fornica.
She looks about as comfortable
as a peacock in our furnace.
She tries hard not to inhale too deeply.
"Brother, put down your sword."

Andrea sheathes his metal
but keeps his hand on the grip.

Leona fans herself
with a large document.
"Giovanna and I have been
examining the will all morning
and may have found a solution
to our dilemma. Nowhere does
the will state the first names
of Giovanna or Maria
but only refers
to the first and second daughters
of Angelo Barovier."

I shrug.
"But, Leona, everyone knows
that Giovanna is the elder
and I am the younger daughter, so—"

Leona rolls her eyes
and raises her hand to me,
annoyed as only an older sister can be.
"That would be a problem only
were you not to marry a nobleman, Maria.
And the betrothal papers drawn between
the Bembo family and the Barovier family
state only that a daughter of Angelo Barovier
is to marry my brother."

Like three singing larks, Andrea,
Luca, and Vanna look about to rejoice
in heavenly praise.

"I don't understand." And I don't.

"Dearest Maria," Andrea says.
"All you must do is marry a nobleman
according to your father's will.
You need not marry me. And I must
only marry a daughter Barovier,
not specifically you.
For we have not been ringed."

Andrea smiles an ocean's breadth
at my sister. So he does wish
to marry her after all.

I clutch the finished betrothal glass
to my chest, almost to crushing it.
I had a similar plan but now wish
never to admit it.

"What do you hold there?" Luca asks.
"Please let us see."

I would give it up to no one,
but his plea is sweeter than sugared figs.

Leona examines the glass,
eyes me oddly, then laughs.
"You silly girl. You had the same plan."

"Only I will throw myself
to sea before I marry a nobleman
I do not love," I say indignantly.

A NOBLEMAN'S CLEVER SOLUTION

Andrea clears his throat.
"That may not be necessary, little sister.
For if Luca does not know his surname,
could it not be Bembo?"
Andrea winks at us.
"I believe I have just been reunited
with my long-lost cousin Luca Bembo."

He lets go his sword's handle
and embraces Luca.
"I shall throw a feast of grandeur
two days hence to anoint you, Luca Bembo,
and welcome you home."

Andrea is so tall and handsome
right now I should like to smother him
with kisses, but I wisely leave
that privilege to my sister.
Vanna gives Andrea her hand
and he seals it a hundred times over
with his lips.

GOD'S WILL

Mother awaits me in my chambers
with my dancing master,
who has been hired
to lead me through the streets
as we publicly announce
my engagement to Andrea tomorrow.

"Mother, an urgent matter
calls your attention in the hall,"
I say, and nearly drag her like
a tugboat from my room
until she and the master follow me.

Mother is shocked
to see Andrea, Leona, Luca,
Vanna, Uncle Giova, and my brothers
stand before her.
Uncle Giova beckons
her to assume her rightful chair at the table.
It appears as though as we are
about to coronate Mother queen.

Uncle Giova makes our plea,
and the dancing master
cannot control his feet.
The master clicks his heels.
"Highly unusual. But what
a beautiful procession of gondolas
this will make, double the number of boats.
The elder sister dancing before
the clumsy younger one.
I have never before seen it.
It will be the rage of Venice."

Mother interrupts him.
"I have yet to give my consent."
Her eyes hold back tears.
Mother weighs this as though she
were determining whether
to send Vanna and me to war.
She crosses herself and calls
me and my sister to kneel
at her side, gathering our hands
in hers. "I hope my decision is just.
Your father always said,
'God's will will out.'
You shall both go forth
and marry as you choose.
I believe in my heart this
is God's will,
and no will of man
should interfere with that."

WHAT TO DO ABOUT MY FATHER'S WILL

For a wedding gift
Luca gives my sister and Andrea
all of the ducats of my dowry.

I clutch the paper
that holds Father's original
recipe for cristallo.

Father believed, with the conviction
of a stubborn child
who will not come in from the cold,
that when he invented clear glass,
it was God's will to reward me
with a husband,
even though in his heart
he knew Vanna
was best suited for a senator.
If only he had lived longer.

For I know that if he
were alive today,
he would want us to create
these unions,
that he would see with clarity
how happy Vanna and I are
and rejoice.

SISTERS OF GLASS

I do not want the waving to end,
but Vanna's gondola grows smaller
until it is but a speck
on the horizon.

Luca's ringed hand clasps mine.
"It is not as though
you shall not see Giovanna.
You will visit your aunts
in the convent two weeks hence.
So why this ocean of tears?"

"Because she was made for Venice
and I for Murano,
and I will be so lonely
here without her," I say.

"What is it that she can do
that I cannot for you?" Luca asks.

"Well, for one thing, she sang
to me while I prepared the batch?"

Luca opens his mouth,
and a horrible honk
like a sickly goose emerges.

"Please save your tunes
for the blowpipe, my love.
I shall have singing enough in mass."

We both laugh.

"There is only one Vanna," Luca says.

"Do you suppose she misses me?" I ask him.

"I am certain that right now, instead
of marveling as she should, as any girl should,
about her good fortune
in taking such a dashing husband,
she is lamenting the fact
that you will not be around
to sketch for her.
Oh, Maria, will you never be satisfied?"

I shrug.

"Well, my dear. Close your eyes now
and I shall give you your wedding gift."

Luca leads me from my mother's palazzo
into the road. I feel the last stretch of sun
upon my face. And before I can orient myself,
Luca spins me round like a child's game.

"This is foolish," I say.

When I open my eyes,
we stand in the second fornica.
The furnace is repaired, only it differs
slightly from our first fornica.
"What is that oven over there
and those tools?" I ask.

"I thought that with your talent
at sketching, you might try enameling
while I blow glass. We could then
work together."

I am stunned, still and silent as a wall.

"Oh, you hate it.
You need never work, Maria.
I just thought—"

I stutter. "I . . . love . . . it. I just don't
know what to say."

"Well, that is a new proposition.
Maria Barovier without words."
Luca smiles.
"Well, then kiss me, you foolish girl."

And so, I do.

GLOSSARY

annealer—an oven that is generally heated to about 900 degrees Fahrenheit and used to cool the glass slowly. Overnight, the oven is brought to room temperature so that the glass does not crack from stress.

batch—the mixture of raw components that is used to make glass.

beaker—a glass used for drinking during the Renaissance. It may be made of clear glass and decorated with colorful enamel and gold leaf to signify special occasions.

bella—Italian for "beautiful."

bench—the place where the gaffer works the piece and where all the tools are kept. It has two rails perpendicular to the seat on which the glass pipes are rolled.

Berlingozzo—a simple, ring-shaped cake that was popular for Carnevale in the late fifteenth century. Its name may derive from the word *Berlingaccio*, meaning "Fat Thursday."

betrothal goblet—a vessel made during the courtship and marriage process in Renaissance times, often of Venetian enameled and gilded glass. It was not an item that was used for drinking, but rather a keepsake, commissioned for the special occasion of marriage. Sometimes it contained profiles of the bride and groom.

biretta—a type of headdress composed of three or four rigid sections and a tassel that evolved in the Middle Ages among the cultured classes and the ecclesiastical hierarchies. The felt biretta that was very much in fashion was often yellowish in color. A hat resembling the black biretta continues to be used in courtrooms by judges and lawyers.

bits—tiny scraps of glass that can be added to the mixture to give color, texture, or shape to the glass.

blocks—hand-sized wooden molds used in the early stages of glass shaping.

blowpipe—a hollow steel rod with a mouthpiece at one end that the gaffer blows through to create a bubble in the glass.

bolognini—a unit of currency equal to 1/100 of a ducat.

buon giorno, signore—Italian for "Good day, sir."

camicia—a slip, shift, or chemise that was worn underneath women's garments, generally coming to about mid-calf and made of fine linen. The word *camicia* means "shirt" in Italian.

capon—a castrated rooster or meat from a castrated rooster. It is especially tender and much less stringy than chicken.

cardinal—the highest church official in the city of Venice in the fifteenth century. He wielded great political and social influence and, with a conclave of other cardinals across Italy, chose the next pope.

Carnevale mask—Carnevale is a festival in Venice that is celebrated before the Lenten season (from two weeks before Ash Wednesday until Fat Tuesday, or Mardi Gras) during which masks are worn, making it impossible to distinguish between the social classes. The three most common types of masks are bautas, which can cover the whole face; morettas, which are oval masks of black velvet generally worn to visit the convents; and voltos (also called larvas), which mean "faces" and are the simplest and most common type of mask.

conciatore—a person who prepares a batch.

convent—traditionally, a place where a girl is sent to take up devotions in the Catholic Church and become a nun. However, In the 1400s, the skyrocketing cost of dowries meant that many of the city's noblest families were obliged to place their teenage daughters, regardless of the girls' wishes, in convents. Few of these girls felt a spiritual calling. The nunneries were run like luxury boutique hotels. Novices were given duplicate keys so they could come and go as they pleased from their palatial apartments, which were filled with artwork and overlooked the Grand Canal. Wearing the most fashionable, low-cut dresses, they would entertain male visitors with wine-fueled banquets, then invite their beaux to spend the night in their rooms. They took romantic gondola rides with admirers to private picnics on the islands of the Venice Lagoon and went on poetic moonlit walks in the secluded gardens. The most passionate eloped, presumably with men who were not obsessed with dowries. The mature-age abbesses rode the city in opulent carriages with their pet dogs and oversaw their girls' activities with a maternal eye. If a nun fell pregnant, she would simply give birth in the privacy of the convent and then pass the child off as an orphan abandoned on the doorstep.

Corpus Christi—a Western Catholic feast that honors the Eucharist (the sacrament in which a wafer is eaten during Mass, having become the body and blood of Christ through transubstantiation) and dates back to the thirteenth century. It is celebrated in the Catholic Church on the Thursday following Trinity Sunday, the date of which changes each calendar year.

Council of Ten—one of the major governing bodies of the Republic of Venice from 1310 to 1797. Sometimes known simply as the Ten, the council was formally tasked with maintaining the security of the republic and preserving the government from overthrow or corruption, though its actions were often secretive. The council's small size and rapid ability to make decisions led to its increasing power, and by 1457 the Ten was enjoying almost unlimited authority over all governmental affairs. In particular, it oversaw Venice's diplomatic and intelligence services, managed its military affairs, and handled legal matters and enforcement, including sumptuary laws. The council also attempted, though largely ineffectively, to combat vice.

courtesan—the word originally comes from "courtier," which means "someone who attends a monarch or other powerful official at court." In the Renaissance, *cortigiana* came to mean "the ruler's mistress," and then to mean "a well-educated and independent woman of free morals, a trained artisan of dance and singing, who associated with wealthy, upper-class men who provided luxuries and status in exchange for companionship."

cristallo—a totally clear glass, like rock crystal. Cristallo is thought to have been invented around 1450, with Angelo Barovier often credited as its first inventor.

crucible—the cauldron that holds the glass inside the furnace.

cullet—the hot, molten state of glass when it is being formed in the furnace. Also, the pieces of glassware that have chips that can be broken down and used instead of batch to make glass.

dancing master—the person who led the bride on a procession through the streets and taught various group dances to those in attendance. He also acted as a sort of unofficial modern-day wedding coordinator.

doge—the head of the government in fifteenth-century Venice.

dowry—the money, goods, or estate that a woman brings to her husband in marriage.

Ducal Palace—the palazzo on San Marco Piazza where the Doge lived and where the political institutions of the Republic of Venice were housed until the Napoleonic era.

ducat—the most valuable Italian currency during the fifteenth century. It was a small gold coin with the Doge's picture on it.

enameler—one who practices the glass art of enameling. Enamel is a material made by fusing powdered glass to a substrate by firing, usually at between 1380 and 1560 degrees Fahrenheit, until the powder melts, flows, and then hardens to a smooth, durable vitreous coating on metal, glass, or ceramic. Frit is also often used in enameling. The fired enameled ware is a fully laminated composite of glass and metal.

fornica—Italian for "furnace," the location where glassblowing takes place. This oven holds liquid glass and is usually heated to about 2000 to 2200 degrees Fahrenheit.

frit—the hard substance the glass becomes as it is formed. Also, tiny chips of glass that can be used in the coloring process.

gaffer—a glassblower.

gilder—someone who performs gilding, a decorative technique wherein gold leaf or silver is applied to surfaces such as wood, metal, or stone.

gondola—a traditional, flat-bottomed rowing boat, well suited to the conditions of the Venetian Lagoon. For centuries, gondolas were the chief means of transportation and the most common watercraft within Venice.

jacks—large tongs that are used to create scores in the neck of a piece of glass. It is often the main tool used by glassblowers.

lip—the top edge of the piece of glass.

maestro—an Italian glass master.

manganese—a metal that helps keep the glass clear and pure. Known as "glassblowers' soap," it's the third ingredient used in making the mixture for a batch of cristallo.

marver—a marble table that is used to roll and shape the glass.

mi rifiuto—Italian for "I refuse."

moile—the blob of molten glass that is on the steel blowpipe or punty.

Murano—a series of islands off the northeast coast of Venice best known for glassblowing. In 1291, the Venetian government moved the glassblowing industry to Murano, purportedly to prevent fires but also to control its most profitable industry.

neck—the edge of a piece of glass that will be scored and separated when it is transferred to the punty.

paddle—a wooden tool that flattens the bottom of a piece of glass.

palazzo—a palace or large house.

Piazza San Marco—(St. Mark's Square) generally known as the Piazza, the political, social, and religious center and principal square of Venice. In the fifteenth century, the bricked pavement would have been laid, the Doge's palace would have been part of the square (or what is known as the Piazzetta), and St. Mark's Basilica would have existed as well.

pincers—a tool that can be used to develop glass, to fix handles, and to form the spout on jugs. Pincers are also used to guide the color patterns, to manipulate the shape of the glass, and to open the piece by hand.

podesta—the political leader or chief magistrate of an Italian city-state. The political leader of Murano in the fifteenth century.

punty/pontil—the solid metal rod a glassblower uses for bits and to transfer glass from the blowpipe.

Rialto Bridge—the oldest bridge across the Grand Canal in Venice. The stone bridge that you see today was designed by Antonio da Ponte and finished in 1591, so at the time of this book, the Rialto Bridge would have been made of wood. One of the wood versions of the bridge had collapsed in 1444, but the one that existed in 1465 would have looked remarkably similar to the stone version that you see standing today.

ricordare—Italian for "remember."

rosary—from the Latin for "garland of roses," a Catholic devotion. The rosary is a necklace of prayer beads that is used to count a series of prayers—Our Father, Hail Mary, and Glory Be to the Father—along with praying one of now twenty mysteries of the rosary.

senator—one who wore red robes and served as part of the government of the Republic of Venice. Senators came from the aristocracy. The end of the fifteenth century saw the beginning of the golden book of senators, meaning that your family name had to be written in a special book of old, long-standing aristocratic Venetian nobility for you to become a senator.

shears—a scissors-like tool that is used to cut a straight line or bit of glass.

signore—Italian for the polite address for a man.

sorella—Italian for "sister."

tweezers—a tool used to pinch and pull glass.